Littlest PetShop™

TRADING CARDS

VOLUME 1

MALTESE
"Don't hate me for bein cuter than you are."
SCHOLASTIC

DALMATIAN
"Which way to the firehouse?"
SCHOLASTIC

SCOTTIE
"Has anyone seen my bagpipes?"
SCHOLASTIC

SCHOLASTIC INC.

New York   Toronto   London   Auckland   Sydney
Mexico City   New Delhi   Hong Kong   Buenos Aires

ISBN-13: 978-0-545-03434-0
ISBN-10: 0-545-03434-5

LITTLEST PET SHOP is a trademark of Hasbro and is used with permission. © 2007 Hasbro. All Rights Reserved. Published by Scholastic Inc. SCHOLASTIC and associated logos are trademarks and/or registered trademarks of Scholastic Inc.

Licensed by Hasbro

12 11 10 9 8 7 6 5 4 3 2 1   7 8 9 10/0

Printed in the U.S.A.
First printing, September 2007

TRADE YOUR CARDS!

This book contains **81** fabulous trading cards, each featuring one of the Littlest Pet Shop pets. Punch them out and figure out which pets are in your collection. You can fill in the backs of those cards with details about each pet. You can trade the cards with your friends, or keep them all for yourself!

GET CRAFTY!

You can make your very own personalized album to hold your card collection.

Here's what you'll need:

- One 3-ring binder
- Nine 9-pocket plastic storage sleeves (these will have three holes punched in the side so that you can insert them into the 3-ring binder)
- Puffy paint or fabric paint

If you like, you can use these things as well:

- Pretty scraps of material or ribbon
- Fabric glue
- Photos of your pet collection
- Stencil letter stickers

Here's what you do:

Insert the plastic sleeves in the 3-ring binder. Organize your cards any way you like by slipping each one into a pocket. You can put them in order alphabetically, by pet type, or according to when you adopted each pet! Then decorate the front, spine, and back of the binder. You can use puffy paints or fabric paints, or cover the binder with a pretty piece of material or some ribbon using the fabric glue. You can also glue a photo of your pet collection to the front of the binder, or use stencil letter stickers to give your album a cool name!

LISTMANIA!

Which are your favorite pets? Fill in these "Top 10" lists!

TOP 10 MOST FAVE DOGS

1. _____
2. _____
3. _____
4. _____
5. _____
6. _____
7. _____
8. _____
9. _____
10. _____

TOP 10 MOST ADORABLE CATS

1. _____
2. _____
3. _____
4. _____
5. _____
6. _____
7. _____
8. _____
9. _____
10. _____

TOP 10 MOST FABULOUS PETS

1. Dog
2. Cat
3. monkey
4. _____
5. _____

6. _____
7. _____
8. _____
9. _____
10. _____

GAME TIME!

If you take a look at your Littlest Pet Shop trading cards, you'll notice that each card is one of five colors: pink, **purple**, blue, green, or yellow. That means it's easy to use your entire set of trading cards like a deck of cards! Get together with a group of friends and try playing this fun game.

Here's how to set up:

Punch out all the cards and shuffle them (be sure to remove the "Littlest Pet Shop" card from the deck). Distribute eight cards to each player. Place the rest of the cards facedown in a pile in the middle of the table. Turn the top card over and create a new "discard" pile. You're ready to play!

Here's how to play:

You can play with 2 to 8 players. The youngest player gets to go first. That player has to match either the color or the pet type of the card on top of the "discard" pile. For example, if the card is purple and the pet is a dog, the player can only place another purple card OR a dog card of another color on top. If the player doesn't have either, she must pick another card from the "draw" pile. If she can play the card she's just picked, she should, but if not, play moves to the person sitting to her left. The first player to discard all her cards wins!

ULTIMATE CROSSWORD

ACROSS

4. A photographer mouse might want you to say this when you smile.
5. A princess kissed this pet and he turned into a prince!
6. This pet knows that slow and steady wins the race.
7. Birds of a _____ flock together.
8. A kitten who sleeps takes one of these.

DOWN

1. Goldfish love this card game.
2. This dog loves bagpipe music.
3. Restaurant leftovers come in this.

BEAGLE

"Heard any good gossip?"

■Scholastic

POODLE

"Bonjour!"

■Scholastic

CHIHUAHUA

"Can I borrow your sweater?"

■Scholastic

PUG

"I'm such a romantic."

■Scholastic

COCKER SPANIEL

"I should have been a professional singer."

■Scholastic

BOXER

"Let's be friends."

■Scholastic

SCOTTIE

"I've got my stylist on speed dial."

■Scholastic

GERMAN SHEPHERD

"I'll protect you!"

■Scholastic

PLAYFUL PUPPY #1

"Let's go to the dog park."

■Scholastic

First name

Middle name

Last name

Date of adoption

Favorite food

Favorite color

Favorite toy

First name

Middle name

Last name

Date of adoption

Favorite food

Favorite color

Favorite toy

First name

Middle name

Last name

Date of adoption

Favorite food

Favorite color

Favorite toy

First name

Middle name

Last name

Date of adoption

Favorite food

Favorite color

Favorite toy

First name

Middle name

Last name

Date of adoption

Favorite food

Favorite color

Favorite toy

First name

Middle name

Last name

Date of adoption

Favorite food

Favorite color

Favorite toy

First name

Middle name

Last name

Date of adoption

Favorite food

Favorite color

Favorite toy

First name

Middle name

Last name

Date of adoption

Favorite food

Favorite color

Favorite toy

First name

Middle name

Last name

Date of adoption

Favorite food

Favorite color

Favorite toy

CAT

"Wanna go for a run?"

SCHOLASTIC

LONG-HAIRED CAT

"Who's up for a movie?"

SCHOLASTIC

CAT

"Will someone braid my ponytail?"

SCHOLASTIC

SHORT-HAIRED CAT

"My pen is out of ink again."

SCHOLASTIC

SIAMESE CAT

"Diamonds are a cat's best friend."

SCHOLASTIC

LONG-HAIRED CAT

"Hi-ya!"

SCHOLASTIC

PERSIAN CAT

"I'd rather be napping."

SCHOLASTIC

LONG-HAIRED CAT

"Let's go get a makeover."

SCHOLASTIC

CALICO CAT

"Does my outfit match?"

SCHOLASTIC

First name

Middle name

Last name

Date of adoption

Favorite food

Favorite color

Favorite toy

First name

Middle name

Last name

Date of adoption

Favorite food

Favorite color

Favorite toy

First name

Middle name

Last name

Date of adoption

Favorite food

Favorite color

Favorite toy

First name

Middle name

Last name

Date of adoption

Favorite food

Favorite color

Favorite toy

First name

Middle name

Last name

Date of adoption

Favorite food

Favorite color

Favorite toy

First name

Middle name

Last name

Date of adoption

Favorite food

Favorite color

Favorite toy

First name

Middle name

Last name

Date of adoption

Favorite food

Favorite color

Favorite toy

First name

Middle name

Last name

Date of adoption

Favorite food

Favorite color

Favorite toy

First name

Middle name

Last name

Date of adoption

Favorite food

Favorite color

Favorite toy

HAMSTER

"I keep running, even if I never get anywhere."

■SCHOLASTIC

MOUSE

"Got anything to nibble on?"

■SCHOLASTIC

HAPPY HAMSTER #1

"Who's ready for a workout?"

■SCHOLASTIC

HAPPY HAMSTER #2

"Who wants to go down the slide again?"

■SCHOLASTIC

HAPPY HAMSTER #3

"Aren't we the cutest critters?"

■SCHOLASTIC

BUNNY

"Hop to it!"

■SCHOLASTIC

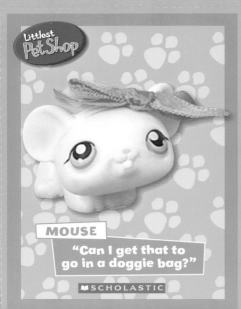

MOUSE

"Can I get that to go in a doggie bag?"

■SCHOLASTIC

BUNNY

"Can I have one of your treats?"

■SCHOLASTIC

GUINEA PIG

"Want to cuddle?"

■SCHOLASTIC

First name

Middle name

Last name

Date of adoption

Favorite food

Favorite color

Favorite toy

First name

Middle name

Last name

Date of adoption

Favorite food

Favorite color

Favorite toy

First name

Middle name

Last name

Date of adoption

Favorite food

Favorite color

Favorite toy

First name

Middle name

Last name

Date of adoption

Favorite food

Favorite color

Favorite toy

First name

Middle name

Last name

Date of adoption

Favorite food

Favorite color

Favorite toy

First name

Middle name

Last name

Date of adoption

Favorite food

Favorite color

Favorite toy

First name

Middle name

Last name

Date of adoption

Favorite food

Favorite color

Favorite toy

First name

Middle name

Last name

Date of adoption

Favorite food

Favorite color

Favorite toy

First name

Middle name

Last name

Date of adoption

Favorite food

Favorite color

Favorite toy